HUEY TH
RED CAR

and his Mysterious Passenger

LOUISE BANDS is the mother of three grown sons and the grandmother of five. She is a teacher whose stories are always in demand. Her father was a geologist and her early life was spent in the Kalahari Desert in South Africa. A keen observer of the world around her and an avid reader, she has been writing poems and stories since she was eleven years old.

The first of the Huey stories was told to amuse a class of children in a small country school in Scotland, where she and her husband, Michael, a retired clergyman, live. The children enjoyed the story so much Louise was asked to produce a new one each week. This little collection is a sample of what the children wanted - their magic lies in the fact that they were created for and assessed - and approved by children.

HUEY THE LITTLE RED CAR

and his Mysterious Passenger

LOUISE BANDS

Illustrations by Michael Bands

 **New Generation Publishing**

Huey

*For all the delightful children I have taught in the
past ten years in Scotland - especially the little
people of Brydekirk Primary School.*

CONTENTS

**1. HUEY AND THE LORRY FULL OF
   LOGS**   **9**

2. HUEY'S NEW WHEELS   **16**

3. HUEY AND THE POLICE   **23**

4. HUEY AT THE BRIDGE   **33**

5. HUEY AND THE HORSE BOX   **39**

6. HUEY GETS A SURPRISE   **45**

**7. HUEY AND THE LITTLE RED
   SQUIRREL**   **52**

8. THE CHRISTMAS TALE   **59**

THE FIRST ADVENTURE

HUEY AND THE LORRY FULL OF LOGS

I bought this little red car, you see - not red like a fire engine, and not red like a tomato, but red like a delicious, ripe plum. He was small and neat and easy for me to drive because I'm quite small too. I called him "Huey" because his registration was SA 52 UHE. You see? U-HE, or "Huey."

Huey used to belong to a friend of mine. Nan was a very dear and wise old lady, and when I came to live in Scotland, she became my very best friend. When she was young, she had lived in Africa as I had. She had three sons, just as I have three sons, and she used to be a teacher too.

Whenever I was feeling tired or lonely or worried about school, I would go to visit Nan. She would make tea for us, and she always had good things to eat in her cake tins - shortbread, chocolate biscuits, ginger biscuits, fruit cake, or mince pies at Christmas, and hot-cross buns at Easter. Then she would light the fire in the sitting room, and we would settle down with our tea, served in beautiful cups with blue roses on them, and we would have a good chat.

When it was time for me to go home, she would walk with me to the corner of the road, where there is a lamppost, and there we would say good-bye. She would give me a hug and a little kiss. She always wore a lovely, delicate perfume that smelled like a garden in summer - full of flowers. Long after I'd left Nan, I could still smell her perfume, a gentle reminder that my friend was still with me, if only in my thoughts.

I didn't get Huey straight after Nan died. He was left on his own, in the road outside her house, and one night, some local lads kicked off (and stole) his left front wheel trim. Poor Huey looked so sad, like someone who has a tooth missing. So her sons drove him around and parked him in my garden. We took care of Huey for many months, while they decided what to do with him. Eventually, they agreed that I could buy him. It took a long time for all the new papers to be signed and a new licence to be bought, but one day, Huey was mine. I could clean him and polish him. We bought a new wheel trim for him and parked him in my garage, where the naughty boys could not steal his new wheel trim!

I loved driving Huey. He was new and clean and smart, and despite the fact that his engine was only tiny - smaller than one litre - he zipped willingly along the country roads.

Then a strange thing began to happen. The first time, I was driving to Lochmaben one day, and I could smell Nan's perfume in the car with me. There was nothing of Nan's in the car. Was it possible that her perfume could have lingered in the car for such a long time? It was strange, but it didn't worry me. I loved Nan, and it was nice to be reminded of her. On many days when I would drive around, the scent wasn't there. Then, suddenly, one day it would be back! When I could smell it, I always had a warm, good feeling that Nan was somewhere near.

I was driving to school one dreary, wet

morning, when an extraordinary and unexplainable thing happened. Huey's wipers were whizzing at full speed, battling bravely to keep the rain off the windscreen. The road was full of puddles the size of lakes, and I was late for school. I was driving Huey as fast as I dared, ploughing through the water that was washing up beside us, and trying desperately to see out of the rain-splattered windows. Blast it! There was a tractor in front of me on the road, yellow lights flashing and water spraying high from under his huge wheels. I would have to pass him! I was late for school! I could not see a thing in the road ahead. Should I take a chance and pull out and overtake it, even though I couldn't see if the road was clear? I slowed down behind the tractor, beating the steering wheel with the palms of my hands in frustration. What should

I do? I would chance it! I changed gears, revved the engine, and began to pull out when . . . Suddenly, I became aware of Nan's perfume - strongly with me - and I thought I heard her voice saying, "Careful! Be careful. There's a lorry coming!"

I braked hard and swung back in behind the tractor. Seconds later, a huge lorry, piled high with logs, came out of the mist and passed me, nearly drowning Huey with the tidal waves of water it sprayed up!

I was stunned. It would have been a most awful crash - it would have pushed the tractor off the road, squashed Huey into a sardine tin, and most certainly killed me! I slowed and stopped Huey on the side of the road. I put my head down on my hands on the steering wheel and took some very deep breaths. And then I said, "Thank you, Nan. Thank you!"

I got to school safely, not too late, and all through the day, I kept thinking about this most astonishing thing that had happened that morning.

By now Huey and I have been travelling together for many months. Sometimes Nan travels with us, sometimes she doesn't. I always know when she's there - I can smell her perfume. We have had many adventures together - Nan and Huey and I - but those tales, I'll tell you another day!

HUEY'S NEW WHEELS

Huey had to go to the garage. When I was filling him up with petrol recently, the kindly garage mechanic had a look at his back wheels.

"You'll be needing some new back tyres soon," he said. "Look at this."

He took a match out of his pocket and put it on one of Huey's back tyres. He put it into the groove of the tyre, but it fell out.

"You see," he said, "the grooves, or tread, as we call it, must be deeper than this matchstick. Otherwise, the tyres are illegal. That means you'll be in trouble with the police if they find out!"

Oh dear, we didn't want to be in trouble with the police. So the next day, I went to the tyre exchange and made an appointment for Huey to have his new tyres fitted at the end of the week.

We had to be at the tyre exchange bright and early on that morning. I parked Huey in one of the bays and handed the keys in at the office.

"We'll phone you as soon as the job is done," the cheerful tyre man told me.

It seemed hardly any time at all had passed before the phone rang and they said Huey was ready. I walked up to the tyre exchange and drove Huey home with two brand new tyres.

The following Monday, Huey and I had to be at a big school quite far from home. It was a long way to go, so we went on the motorway. Motorway driving is always a bit scary, as Huey is small, and there are so many huge lorries, and all the smart black and gleaming silver cars are so fast. Their front grills look like big shiny teeth, and the cars seem to say, "Move over little Huey; you're too small and slow. We're important, and we're in a hurry!"

We tried to look as brave as we could as we zipped along at seventy miles per hour.

When school was over, the sun was shining, and everything was clean and bright after the rain. It was a splendid afternoon, and we didn't need to hurry, so we took the long way home, through the country lanes. This was much more fun than the motorway! I opened Huey's windows to let the clean, sweet-smelling air blow in, and I sang as we drove along.

{Song}

Over the hills and far away,

Huey's going home at last.

We like the lanes on a sunny day,

The motorway is much too fast!

I was making such a noise with my singing that it was a long time before I noticed a strange noise following me along the road. It was a funny "whap-whap-whap" sound. *Whatever could it be?* I closed the window and the sound was softer. I opened the window, and the noise grew louder. I slowed down, and the noise slowed down. I speeded up, and the noise speeded up. How funny. It was definitely following me. What on earth could it be? I was wondering what to do when I got that now-familiar whiff of perfume.

"Okay, Nan," I said softly. "What's up?"

"Pull over and stop," came a quiet voice. "Look at your left back wheel."

So I did just that. I found a safe place to stop. I

got out and walked around Huey, looking at the wheels. Nothing. I couldn't see anything. How odd. I kicked the wheels, but nothing moved. Well, I couldn't stay here all day. I got back in and drove off again. The noise came back. Whap-whap-whap! Whatever it was, I'd better go slowly. So Huey and I limped home at twenty miles per hour, going whap-whap-whap all the way. I still had the window open, and the afternoon was still shining and smelling sweetly of clover and hay, but I didn't feel like singing any more.

In the silence, I heard that small voice say, "Go to the tyre exchange." So as soon as I got to town, I drove straight to the tyre exchange.

The cheery man came out. "What can I do for you today?" he asked.

I told him about the funny noise. He took Huey

into the workshop and fitted some strange device onto each of his wheels in turn. Right front, okay. Left front, okay. Right back, uh-oh, a bit loose, but not too bad. Left back, good grief! It was only just holding on. All the nuts in the wheel were as loose as could be! The wheel was just about to fall off! They had forgotten to tighten the nuts properly when they had changed Huey's wheels the week before.

The cheery man was not so cheery now. "Sorry," he said. "Do come back again if you're not satisfied."

I won't ever go there again, I thought as I drove away.

Then I remembered the motorway. What on earth would I have done if Huey's wheel had come off while we were speeding along between the fast cars and the huge lorries?! I realized what a terrible accident there could have been. *The stuff of nightmares*, I thought as I clutched Huey's steering wheel with shaking hands. Oh how lucky we had been! What would we do without Nan! "Thank you again, Nan!"

HUEY AND THE POLICE!

Late again! Huey and I were rushing to get to school. I always intended to leave with plenty of time to spare but, somehow, it never seemed to work - I seemed to run late a lot. As we sped along, I was thinking of all the things I planned to do with the children that day. I was not aware that the speedometer was climbing steadily. Fifty miles per hour... sixty... sixty-five. We were travelling too fast, over the speed limit!

Suddenly, there it was, that faint whiff of perfume. This was very unusual that it came so early in the morning. However, I had realized from prior experience that it meant that there was some kind of message for me. It could be important.

"What's up, Nan?" I asked.

"Slow down. Now! Slow down!" came the reply.

I had no idea what was going on, but I obediently took my foot off the accelerator and began to brake. Sixty-five, sixty miles per hour. I rounded the corner just beyond the cemetery, and to my horror, there was a police car, bright yellow and blue stripes gleaming in the sunshine, and not one, but two, policemen standing next to it, waving me over into the lay-by.

I did a quick, panic-stricken check: Yes, I had remembered to wear my glasses; yes, I was wearing my seatbelt! Thank goodness I had slowed down!! "Thank you, Nan." *Why were they stopping me?*

I pulled over and stopped.

The policemen came up and started to walk around Huey. They looked awfully serious! The first one was a very large man, and the luminous vest he was wearing made him look even bigger. He had a droopy moustache and his cap was pulled low over his eyes. The second one was smaller. I noticed his vest had one stripe missing and he had a funny left eye. They motioned for me to open the window.

"Where are you going?" asked the big officer, as the smaller one began to circle around Huey.

I felt a bit stupid to be going to school at my age, but I answered truthfully. "To school." And then I added, just in case, "Please don't make me late!"

"May I see your driver's licence, please," continued the large man.

Oh help! I did not have it with me. Then I remembered I had a photocopy of my licence in my schoolbag. I rummaged through it. Thank goodness, there it was. I handed it through the window, holding my breath. He looked at it for some time and then handed it back to me. Meanwhile, the little fellow was still circling Huey.

"Turn on your headlights," he instructed me. I did as I was told.

"Now the left indicator," he barked. Click-click went the indicator.

"Now the right one." Click-click again. He moved around to the back.

"Now the back lights."

Okay, so far, so good.

"Now put your foot on the brake!" he growled.

I braked hard.

"Ah ha!" came the grim voice from behind me. "*Right back brake light is not working!*"

I couldn't believe it. How was I to know it was not working? How could I be behind Huey when I was driving him!

The large man looked solemn and came to the window. He was writing out a pink ticket. This is it, I thought. Huey and I are in trouble!

As he handed me the ticket, he said, "You have twenty-four hours to get that light fixed, and when it is fixed, you have to get the garage to sign this pink paper, with the date and time that they did the job. Then you have to bring this paper to the police headquarters in Dumfries. Do you understand?"

What a fuss and bother about a silly back light. However, I did not dare cheek the policeman. I looked as polite as I could and said, "Could I post it to you instead?"

"Yes, that will be all right," he replied. "Just see that we have it within two weeks. If we don't, you will have to go to court. You will have to pay a very big fine, and we might impound your car."

What! Put Huey in the car pound! It was like putting a person in jail!

"Yes, sir," I murmured meekly. "I will see that it is fixed. May I go now, please?"

"Right," said the large policeman, "Off you go then, and don't let this happen again!"

I put Huey into gear and drove off slowly and carefully. I could see the policemen in my rearview mirror, still watching me.

"Wow, Huey! That was a close shave. We would have been in serious trouble if I had not slowed down. A broken brake light was not as bad as a speeding fine and three points on my licence!"

"You're a star, Nan," I whispered, as we drove along the road to school. "Thank you once again for your help."

After school, I went straight to the garage and got Huey's brake light fixed and the pink slip signed and dated, and then I posted it to the Police Headquarters in Dumfries. I must admit, it was dreadfully scary being stopped by the police, and I wondered if my friends were in any of the passing cars. They would be wondering what on earth I had done wrong. Why had I been stopped by the police? It did teach me a good lesson. I am much more careful about keeping to the speed limit now.

After the scary incident with the police, I wrote a new song for Huey to remind us to stick to the rules of the road. I have written it out, as I think it

would be a good reminder for all of us!

HUEY'S SONG

(AFTER BEING STOPPED BY THE POLICE)

Ha Hum Hippity Hoo,

These are the things that Huey must do.

Don't drive too fast - don't be speedy!

Keep to the left and don't be greedy.

Ha Hum Hippity Hoo,

These are the things that Huey must do.

Don't overtake if you can't see ahead,

And always stop when the lights turn red.

Ha Hum Hippity Hoo,

These are the things that Huey must do.

Follow the rule that says "buckle up"!

Don't talk on your mobile - don't be a yup.

Ha Hum Hippity Hoo,

These are the things that Huey must do.

Don't fiddle and fuss when you're on the road.

Don't squeeze in too many - don't overload.

Ha Hum Hippity Hoo,

These are the things that Huey must do.

If you keep to these rules, you'll have nothing to fear.

You'll be safe on the road, all through the year.

Ha Hum Hippity Hoo,

These are the things that Huey must do!

HUEY AT THE BRIDGE

It was supposed to be a beautiful day in spring. There were cheerful yellow daffodils nodding their pretty heads in the fields, and here and there, one could see splashes of pink where a tree had put on a frilly skirt of early blossoms. Little golden primroses and pale yellow cowslips snuggled down along the banks of the river.

Huey and I were just about to leave school when the first large drops of rain began to fall. The lovely sunny morning had disappeared, and since break time, the clouds had been banking up along the hill tops. They were dark, ugly clouds that looked like purple bruises. I leaped in and slammed the door.

"This is it, Huey," I said. "If we don't go now, we'll never get home. We'll have to spend the night at school!"

We set off up the hill, with Huey's wipers going to-and-fro, to-and-fro.

Not too bad, I thought. *I'll just take it slowly. These roads can be very slippery when they're wet!* Pretty soon, the rain was falling in huge, wet waves, and I turned the wipers to their fastest speed, but they hardly made any difference. We seemed to be driving into a solid wall of water. We were on the downhill slope to the river. I knew there was a sharp bend in the road, just before the very narrow bridge that crossed the Annan River. It was getting dark now, and I had switched Huey's lights on. We slowed down as we approached the bridge. I saw some lights coming towards me on the other side. They were coming very fast!

"Oh dear!" I said. "That car is going much too fast. It'll never get over the bridge!"

I stopped Huey and watched the lights. They sped towards us, and then suddenly the lights swerved. There was a terrible squeal of brakes and then a HUGE CRASH . . . and then . . . SILENCE. The car had skidded on the wet road and had crashed into the side of the bridge.

I sat in the dark, inside Huey, and listened to the rain drumming on the roof. I realised I had to do something to help, but what could I do? As I sat in the dark, I smelt a <u>strong</u> smell of perfume. Nan was here!

"First, go and check where the car is," said the soft voice.

I went out in the pouring rain with my little torch in my hand. I stumbled along the road to the bridge. I was terrified! What would I find?

There was a big hole in the side of the bridge, and a small blue car was balancing, just on the edge. I'd better not touch the car. It may topple over the edge. I peered through the window. The young man inside had his head on the steering wheel. He wasn't moving.

"Don't touch him," came Nan's soft voice. "Phone for the police and an ambulance," she said.

I slushed through the water back to Huey and got my mobile phone out of my bag. I dialed 999 and spoke to the person on the line. I explained what had happened and where we were.

"We'll be there as soon as we can," the woman said. "Please wait there. We're coming as quickly as we can."

I went back to the car. I noticed the driver's window was smashed. The young man was starting to shiver. I rushed back to Huey and got my travelling rug. Very, very gently, I put the blanket through the window and covered him. There was nothing else I could do, so I went back to Huey. I climbed in and turned on the engine to run the heater for a while. I was wet and very cold. I waited in the dark for ages and ages.

Later, I heard Nan's voice saying, "Put on the hazard lights now."

I pushed the button, and the lights flashed on, off, on, off in the blackness outside. Then I heard the sound of the ambulance and police car coming. The sirens made a horribly loud noise in the dark night.

Soon there were people rushing everywhere. They pulled the blue car back onto the bridge. The paramedics gently lifted the young man onto a stretcher and put him into the ambulance. Its blue light came on, and the wailing trailed off into the distance. A young policewoman came and asked me lots of questions about how the accident had happened. She wanted to know if I was okay to drive home. Then she left as well.

It was all dark and silent again. "Do you think we might get a medal?" I asked Huey as we drove away. If anyone deserves one, it would be Nan!

HUEY AND THE HORSE BOX

Not very long after the accident on the bridge, Huey and I were travelling along the same road. But this time, we were going to Dalton on our way home from school. Just before we got to the bridge, we turned left onto the road to Dalton. It is a lovely drive from the river to Dalton. The road goes through some very pretty woods, and on this bright, sunny Friday afternoon, we were looking forward to a pleasant, quiet journey. The road twists and turns, and there are lots of corners and bumps in it. It is a slow road at the best of times. But I felt a little irritated when we'd gone only a few miles and I saw a horse box in front of us. It was an old wooden box that had been painted blue, and it was being towed by a green jeep. The jeep was also old, and it was very muddy.

We could see the fat brown bottom of a pony in the horse box and two pointy brown ears that flicked every now and then. The driver was going very slowly and carefully along the twisty, bumpy road. Even so, the box was swinging and swaying to-and-fro. It was much too dangerous to try and pass. We just had to be patient and drive slowly along behind the box.

After a while, staring at the back of the box, I realised that the lock was coming undone. Each time the box hit a bump, the bolt came a bit further out.

"Oh dear, this could be very dangerous indeed!"

I had no idea what to do. Clunk. The box bounced over a particularly big bump in the road, the bolt came out completely, and the right-hand side door swung open. As the box swayed along, the door flapped - open and closed, open and closed.

We could clearly see half of the pony now. I was terrified that the pony would fall out of the box. If she fell in front of Huey, we would most certainly drive over her! Each time I tried to pass, the door would swing open, and I'd have to brake and pull back. What on earth could I do?

Then... there it was... that faint whiff of perfume. And Nan said, "Blow your hooter!" (Or, as the Americans would say, "Honk your horn!")

I pressed my hand down hard. *Parp-parp-parp* went Huey's hooter. *Parp-parp-parp*! The driver ignored me. He probably thought I was some rude, impatient driver trying to pass on the very narrow, twisty road. I tried again. *Parp-parp-parp*!

Nothing! What else could I do?

"Put on the hazard lights and hoot!" said Nan.

So I did. I punched the hazard button and blew the hooter for all I was worth. We must have been quite a sight, Huey and I. He was going flash-flash-flash, and I was going *parp-parp-parp* and waving my hand out of the window. The horse box was going sway, clunk, bang as it rattled along.

Eventually, the driver realised what was happening. He slowed down and turned left onto a farm road. He stopped, got out, and came around to the back of the horse box. Fortunately, the pony's halter rope was tied to a ring in the front of the box, and there was a strong wooden bar behind her legs, so she could not have slipped out of the box. However, it was still a very dangerous way to be driving along a public road.

The driver told us the pony's name was Roxy, and he was taking her to a horse show that was being held at Dalton that weekend. He checked that Roxy was okay and then he patted her on her fat little rump and closed the door. This time he made *very* sure that it was firmly shut and locked.

He shook me by the hand and said, "I am very grateful indeed for your help. Please come to tea next Saturday at my farm. It is called Brydekirk Farm. It is three miles back. You'll see the sign just before the crossroad."

Well! You should have seen that tea! I arrived promptly at 3:30 and was taken into the farm's big dining room. The farmer's wife was there, and all the children too. The table was covered with every kind of good thing you could imagine. There were small salmon pastries, piles of fresh sandwiches, scones with homemade strawberry jam and huge dollops of fresh farm cream, crumpets, flapjacks and, best of all, a HUGE chocolate cake with cherries and walnuts on top. What a feast!!

After tea, we went out to the stable to see Roxy. She was happily munching her hay.

As we drove home, I told Huey all about the tea. I felt sorry for him - all he could expect was a gallon or two of petrol in his tank!

HUEY GETS A SURPRISE

It was a beautiful day in June. The sun was shining after the night of rain. The whole world looked sparkly and bright. The trees were a lovely soft green, the sky was a gentle blue, and the first pale pink dog roses were peeping out of the hedgerows.

Huey and I were on our way to Brydekirk School for the day. We were feeling very happy. Brydekirk was one of our favourite schools, and it was almost the end of term and time for our summer holidays.

As we got near to the village of Brydekirk, we saw the old stone bridge across the river. It is a beautiful old bridge, with a humpback and lots of moss growing on the ancient grey stones. We slowed down to cross safely and then stopped to look at the water gurgling and splashing along under the stone arch of the bridge. There were three swans in the river, floating gently along, paddling with their big webbed feet, their long necks looking like question marks, and their big, strong wings folded gracefully on their backs. Some swallows were swooping and diving, just touching the surface of the water with their beaks. A cheeky little wagtail was strutting and wobbling along on the edge of the bridge, showing off his sleek coat of yellow and grey feathers. It was such a splendid sight. We almost forgot we had to go to school.

I was just about to start Huey's engine when something strange, in the woods on the other side of the road, caught my eye. It was just a flash of deep tawny-brown. What on earth could it be? It moved slowly along and then stopped in the shadows. It was too big for a fox and the wrong colour for a badger. It looked like a cat, but it was much too big. I was just about to get out of the car to investigate, when I got a whiff of familiar perfume.

Nan's voice came urgently, "Be careful. Don't get out of the car!"

"It's okay, Nan," I said. "I have enough time before school starts."

"Stay in the car. You're in very great danger!" came the reply.

"Good grief! Here, in Brydekirk?" I said.

"Yes, indeed you are. I recognise it - it's a lioness!" she said frantically.

"Don't be ridiculous, Nan. This is Scotland, not

Africa!" I said laughing and reaching for the handle of the door.

Just then, the large animal came out of the woods and crossed the road towards Huey. IT WAS A LIONESS! I sat quite still in the car, too terrified to move a muscle. The lioness stalked around Huey, sniffing at the cracks of the doors. Her head was level with my window, which fortunately was tightly closed. I could see her great big, golden eyes. She looked at me through the glass! Perhaps she was considering me for a snack! I held my breath, too scared even to breathe. She moved away, and I could hear her sniffing at Huey's back door. She pawed at the back window with paws the size of soup plates.

"Help, Nan! What on earth should I do?" I murmured frantically.

"Dial 999 and tell the police to contact the RSPCA," was the sensible answer. "Then sit very still and say your prayers!"

I did just as Nan had advised. I expected the police to laugh at me, but they told me to sit still and said they would come as fast as they could. I had quite forgotten about the lovely day. I sat in petrified silence for what seemed ages and ages. The lioness got bored with sniffing around Huey's wheels and eventually lay down against the wall of the bridge. Luckily, no other cars were on that stretch of the road so early in the morning.

Eventually, the police car arrived from the town of Annan, five miles away. I watched as they got out of the car. There were two large policemen in uniform and a smaller man dressed in jeans and a T-shirt. He walked up to the lioness and scratched her under the chin. I watched in astonishment!

"Oh, so this is where you've got to," he said to the lioness. "What are you up to, going for a walk by yourself?"

The lioness purred, a deep, rumbling purr, and rubbed her head against the man's hand!

I could not believe my eyes! Then I heard one of the policemen knocking on my window.

"Thank you for finding her," he said. "We have been looking everywhere for her. She escaped from the circus, which is in Annan at the moment. We were so scared that she might be shot by a farmer. Her name is Leila, and she was born in the circus. 'Big Jim' is her trainer. She is quite tame and very friendly!"

A big red and yellow van with "Barnum's Circus" written on its sides arrived. I watched as

Big Jim took Leila by the ear and led her to the van. She jumped in quite happily, and they drove off, waving at us as they left. The policemen said goodbye and also drove away.

What a start to the day! I looked at my watch. I was very late for school.

"Righto, Huey," I said. "We'd better get a move on. And who is going to believe me when I tell them that we are late for school because a lioness stopped us?"

I was quite sure that I heard a soft chuckle as I put Huey into gear and continued over the bridge to school.

HUEY AND THE LITTLE RED SQUIRREL

Huey and I were on our way home from school. It was a beautiful autumn day. The beech trees on either side of the road were wonderful colours. There were red leaves, orange ones, yellow ones, and golden ones. They drifted down in glowing waves. It was like driving through a long, golden tunnel.

We were not in a hurry. It was much more fun to go slowly and look at all the beauty all around us. I sang my little travelling song:

{Song}

Over the hills and far away,

It really is a lovely day.

We love the trees and the gentle breeze,

The bright sunlight and the buzzing bees.

I noticed a small red squirrel on the side of the road. It was a treat to see a red squirrel. They were becoming rather rare. Their grey cousins from down south were coming up to Scotland and taking their food from them and giving them all sorts of dreadful diseases. We were trying very hard to get rid of the grey ones and to encourage the small red ones to stay. This little fellow looked as though he were one of the autumn leaves that had just fallen from a tree. Huey and I slowed down to have a good look at him. Just then, one of those shiny, silver cars like the ones we had seen on the motorway appeared behind us. It was one of those dreadful cars that looked as though it had large gleaming teeth in the front. It whooshed up and began to overtake us just as the little squirrel began to cross to the road.

Oh no! I thought, *Watch out, little squirrel!*

Too late! The silver car hit the red squirrel just as he set off over the road. The car didn't stop. I think he hardly noticed the small animal. I was sure the tiny creature was dead. I drove on slowly. The afternoon was quite ruined for me.

Then I smelt a trace of that lovely perfume and a small voice said, "Stop. Go back. He isn't dead!"

I slammed on the brakes and carefully backed down the road. I drew over to the side and jumped out of the car. The little fellow was lying on the side of the road amongst the shiny leaves. His eyes were shut, and one of his back legs was hanging limply on the ground, but he was breathing!

Good grief, I thought. *What on earth do I do now?*

The quiet voice came back. "Don't pick him up in your hands. Get something from the car."

I raced back to the car and dug around. What did I have? Yes, I had a small towel that I used to wipe the windows with when they got steamed up. I took the towel, folded it into a big square, and very gently lifted the little squirrel up and put him carefully on top of my coat in the car. I stood looking at the poor little thing.

"Okay, Nan. What next?" I asked softly.

"Take him to the vet," came the reply.

I got back into Huey and drove as fast as I dared all the way to the vet's office. I sprang out and ran into the building. Luckily, there were no other patients in the waiting room. I asked the lady at the desk if I could speak to my favorite vet, Hazel. Again I was lucky - Hazel was on duty that day!

We fetched the small body, wrapped in its towel, and took it into the surgery. Hazel very gently examined him. She looked up at me with a big smile.

"I think he is very lucky," she said. "He has a broken leg and is suffering from shock, but I think we will be able to save him. Leave him with me, and I'll see what I can do."

What wonderful news.

Hazel put a splint, as small as a lollipop stick, onto his little leg and bandaged it up carefully. She gave him something to drink, drip-by-drip, from a small eyedropper. Then she gave him an injection of some kind of antibiotic and put him into a warm box that she called an incubator.

"There you, are little fellow," she said. "I am afraid it will take quite a few days before we know how he is getting on. Phone me tomorrow, and I'll give you the news."

I phoned every day for what seemed to be ages and ages, and each time, Hazel told me that he was getting better and better.

Then, at last, one day she said, "I think little red squirrel is ready to go home!"

We drove back to the part of the woods where I had picked him up. Hazel took the small cage out of the car and went a few yards into the woods, away from the road, before she opened it. The little squirrel hopped out, then sat looking around, as if he was not quite sure where he was. Then he bounded off and climbed a tree, quick as a wink. His leg certainly seemed to be working well. I felt really worried about him and wondered if he had found his family again. There was really no way of knowing.

Often, when I drive through that particular patch of beech woods, I think of little red squirrel and wonder how he is getting on. Perhaps the only one who knows is Nan.

THE CHRISTMAS TALE

It was December. There were only a few days left in the year. Everywhere, people were getting ready for Christmas. The shops were full of brightly coloured lights, gaily coloured parcels, and excited shoppers, busy buying presents, while carols floated out every time a door opened and closed.

It had been snowing on and off for a few days - not too much snow, just enough to give a sprinkling of white over everything. The world looked as though someone had dusted it with icing sugar.

Huey and I were at a small school far out in the country. The day had started off with a bit of sunshine. Little patches of light made the snow sparkle and wink at us as we drove along. By lunchtime, however, the sun had disappeared. Squat, dark clouds were hugging the tops of the hills. It was getting darker and darker. Three o'clock came, and the little school was just a small spot of light against the shadows on the hills. Worried parents rushed the children away, to the warmth and safety of their homes on the lonely farms.

"It's going to snow again," they said, looking anxiously at the low, grey clouds.

I hurried through all the last minute things I had to do. I finished marking the children's work and tidied up the classroom. I was anxious to leave as soon as I could. We had a long way to go home, over deserted country roads.

At last I was ready. "Goodnight, Bill," I called to the janitor, who was doing the last checking and locking up before he hurried home too. It was as dark as midnight outside, although it was only four o'clock. I threw my schoolbag onto the back seat and hopped into Huey just as the first big, fluffy snowflakes started whirling down.

At first, the going was easy. All we had to do was follow the tracks left by the cars and Land Rovers of the parents who had come to fetch their children from school. But gradually, the tracks vanished as the snow came down more and more heavily and filled them up. Huey's wipers were on full speed, but it was getting increasingly difficult to see the road. We pressed on, using the hedges on either side to keep us on track. We drove on for what seemed ages, although it must have only been about an hour.

The snow kept falling in enormous, white

sheets. Then, it seemed to be getting lighter, so I speeded up a bit. I was very eager to get home. Bad mistake! I turned a corner too fast. Huey's wheels went into a skid, and helplessly, we slid across the road and into a huge bank of soft snow. We were stuck. I tried to reverse, but Huey's wheels could not get a grip. They just spun around, making deeper holes in the snow.

What ever could we do now? I sat quite still for a few minutes, looking out at a very pale world. The snow was deep, almost up to the windows. I took a few shaky breaths to steady myself, and then I undid my seatbelt and reached into my pocket for my mobile phone. I would have to get help. *At least I'm not hurt*, I thought. *I do hope Huey is okay*. I looked at the screen of the mobile phone, glowing pale green in the darkness of the car. NO SIGNAL!!

"Oh, help!" I felt the panic rising up in my chest. *Keep calm*, I told myself sternly. *The first rule after an accident is "Don't leave your car!"*

In any case, it was too cold to go blundering about in the snow, and I was sure to get lost. I sat still, trying to rein in my galloping thoughts, and then I smelt it - a faint whiff of perfume - we weren't alone. Nan was with us!

Slowly, the quiet voice came to me, as Nan told me what to do.

"Keep warm," she said.

I put on my coat and reached under the seat for the tartan travelling rug I kept there. Soon I was feeling better, less terrified.

"Have a drink."

A cup of hot tea would have been good, but I

drank a little water from the bottle wedged in the door. I must have dozed for a while. I woke up feeling rather hungry.

"Have something to eat," came the small voice.

I remembered a packet of nuts I had in the glove compartment. It helped to pass the time, nibbling away at the nuts. I was getting colder and colder, despite my coat and the blanket. "Turn on the heater for a short while," she said next.

I was very afraid the battery would go flat, but I did as I was told.

"Now turn on the parking lights so that they reflect against the snow."

This is crazy, I thought, but I did it.

Time ticked away slowly. I dozed again in the warmth of the car. I woke feeling fuzzy, so I opened the window a little to let some air in. I thought I heard an engine, very faintly. *Could it be a car?* I listened. There it was again, a faint sound. I thought I saw some lights flickering across the white-out around me.

"Put on the hazard lights," said the little voice.

I fumbled a bit but, found the knob and pressed it. An orange glow flickered ON, OFF, ON, OFF, making weird Halloween patterns on the snow. Yes, there it was again, the sound. It was definitely coming this way! I pushed and shoved until the door opened enough for me to squeeze out, and I stood up, waving my arms. It was a Land Rover, with four large farmers in it. They were going out to check on some of their sheep and had seen the strange orange light flickering on the snow and had come to investigate. I had never been so happy to see anyone in my life! Now all would be well. I opened Huey's door wide and took a deep breath. The hint of perfume had vanished.

"Thank you for keeping us company, Nan," I said, as the farmers began tying ropes onto Huey to pull him out of the snow with their Land Rover.

"Merry Christmas!"

9 781909 593091